the heart's progress

sarah fran wisby

the heart's progress

sarah fran wisby

plain wrap press
san francisco, california

the heart's progress

no copyright 2014 sarah fran wisby

plain wrap press
po box 401153
san francisco, ca

plainwrappress.com

isbn: 978-0-9855976-1-0
library of congress: 2014901742

first plain wrap printing:
february 2014

book design by pernot & tatlin
typeface: urw grotesk pro light

printed in the united states of america

available through Small Press Distribution
spdbooks.org

to RADAR with love

the heart's progress

The heart bears the absence of your mark, but barely. It limps along, an unclaimed parcel, kept alive by licking condensation from the pipes underneath suburban homes and eating the corpses of kamikaze insects that lie fallen in nightly semi-circles under porch lights. Is so much death really necessary to prop up the living? It seems excessive, even gloating, all this insect death. Feigning casualness, the heart glances in windows at night, portals to a sloshing world of ruby toasts over complicated salads. The heart knows *valor* is a too-bright shade of lipstick it can never wear. It creeps away slowly, footfalls going *squish, squish* on the waterlogged lawn.

It goes to the town football field, lies down on the fifty yard line, looks up at stars or the still-traveling light from dead stars, there is no way of knowing which is which, just like there is no way of knowing from a person's eyes when you first meet them whether or not one day they will wish you dead, or whether they will be the one to teach you what you need to know to be really actually alive, even though everything in the universe has already happened and we are just waiting to catch up to it. We must not look like we are waiting, though. We must look like we haven't a care in the world.

The heart goes to 7-11, gets a red bull, cracks it open in the parking lot. A creature worse off than itself rolls by with a shopping cart, dressed entirely in burlap sacks. The heart goes out to it, automatically, then retreats. A symbolic move, like genuflecting, the muscles contracting in place. The overloaded cart has a squeak in one of its wheels: *rheeeeeeeeeeeeeeeeee?* it asks. From deep inside the burlap cave, an answering moan. Faint music from within the convenience store escapes in chilled puffs every time the door opens for another trucker, another cabbie. A bell jingles, festively announcing these customers to the night clerk stocking cups by the hot soup tureen. The heart's drink mumbles softly, gas bubbles colliding with the side of the can. In the quiet night, only these sounds, only these creatures pass each other without pleasure or wonder or fear.

The heart is panting faster now. It scuttles along the highway, turns in circles like a dog flattening imaginary grasses, thinks how far it's come from the days when it couldn't help but pound to Beethoven or catch at the sight of blood. Seeing lights in the distance, not wishing to be seen, running as if to outpace instinct, it makes for a clump of trees, a "forest" along the edge of a golf course. The line between wild and tamed is a plucked string wavering before it breaks entirely. Under the canopy, silence drips from little jets. The heart wishes it were deaf to itself, and could ride silence like an injunction.

The heart likes to say its favorite color is blue, not the blue of the sea or robin's egg blue, not the rich blue of lapis lazuli or of the virgin's robe in countless galleries in Rome, certainly not the dull polyester blue of its school uniform which isn't a color at all but a pronounced lack of color, a preemptive strike against anything the body might choose for itself. The heart says its favorite color is the blue of its own unoxygenated blood, a dark gem swallowed by a dark throat pushing through a velvet maze. *How Morbid*, the other hearts say, *How Ridiculous*, speaking less out of malice than from sheer boredom. Truth is, the heart doesn't trust blue. Blue lies between itself and the world, repairing its nets.

The heart is a frog with a frog in its throat. A misplunked key, a sour note. Did you ever hear a heart murmuring state secrets? Blowing the whistle on white-collar crime? No, the heart only thinks about the heart, the heart, the heart. In school, the heart studies medicine, mathematics, poetry. I have measured out my life in vacu-tubes, the heart beats out on an old Smith-Corona. Every poem the heart writes is meant to be a sort of boomerang, a praise-fetcher, one classmate remarks in workshop. Other classmates concur. Ashamed, the heart drops all classes except archery.

The heart's actual favorite color is vivid red, the color of being seen. Red is a piquant balm for the heart's heart. Where some feel alarm, the heart finds succor. Where some recoil from brutality, the heart cozies up. The heart sleeps best under a quilt of red flags. Every stop sign whispers go.

In archery class, the heart is surprised by how much strength is required to pull back the bow. The entire torso twists and releases. Fingers sprout calluses. Expert archers often have bodies that are developed on one side but not the other. In this and every sport, excessive talent begets monsters. Not that the heart needs to worry. Being naturally lopsided, shaped like a fist sucking its thumb, turns out to be of no advantage. For an entire semester, the heart's arrows only near the target a few times, divoting the paper edge around the bullseye. Still, the heart enjoys practicing this thought: as long as I take aim, no one is taking aim at me, or at least I cannot feel the crosshairs' tiny shadow.

The heart wears billowing sundresses against the heat, big floppy hats and dark glasses to draw attention to its deeply private nature. The heart declares, *I vant to be alone*, like Greta Garbo. Says this to no one in particular, or to its multiplied image in the folded mirrors of the bathroom vanity. Garbo at least was talking to reporters.

The heart is tired of everyone thinking it must be pregnant. "I'm a heart! I'm supposed to be big around the middle!"

Like a prisoner on a chain gang, the heart sorts good love from bad all day long. Sometimes it hides a chunk of love in its sleeve, but it usually falls out by the end of the day.

The heart gets a cheap motel room, hangs up the *do not disturb* sign, locks the door, turns off the lights, unplugs the phone, plugs it back in, calls information, gets the number for suicide prevention, doesn't dial it, unplugs the phone again, closes the blinds, ramps up the air conditioning, strips the sheets, takes a shower, lies dripping atop the stained mattress, staining it a little more, wills itself to stop beating. It lies there for an hour, slowly rising and falling, succeeding in slowing its rate by a fraction of a second. At this rate the heart will die in one million years, or at the end of its natural lifespan, or at an unforeseen time of no one's choosing. It is clear the heart has no control over whether it lives or dies. This is a calming thought, the first in a while. The heart masturbates, then sleeps.

The heart moves to San Francisco, gets a job as a mascot for an internet dating service. At first the heart is elated—it needs no uniform and will be representing something it really believes in. The guy who plays Cupid is totally hot, surfer bod, ringlets, the works, and fortunately wears gold lamé shorts instead of a diaper. They are paid guerrilla theater actors on the cutting edge of advertising. The heart stops rush hour traffic, gets shot by a quiverful of rubber-tipped arrows, stages a die-in. Cupid draws a white chalk-blob around its form, helps it up, and they kiss passionately before taking a bow and handing out flyers. At first the public is responsive. They clutch their own chests when the heart begins its death-waddle. By the kiss they are rolling down their windows and clapping wildly. The heart gets a raise. Things with Cupid are heating up on and off the clock. But the public tires, as publics do. The ads must get bolder and bolder. The heart agrees to skydive off the TransAmerica pyramid while Cupid fires a machine gun from a trolley car, but chickens out at the last minute, gets demoted to an office job. I would've done it, Cupid sneers.

Consider the sounds the heart makes, its slight variations. Sometimes it says *mm-hmm*, sometimes *unh-uh*. If it were a witness speaking from the witness stand, the judge would say *please state yes or no, for the sake of the transcription.*

The heart wears a cloak of shit, eats out of a skull. Few recognize its holiness.

The heart believes in reincarnation. Lessons you spurn in this life will come back in the next. Basically what this means is that no one gets to rest.

The heart works its fingers to the bone, earns enough for a paid vacation. The heart goes to Mexico, to a curved white beach where sea turtles lay their eggs. One night, walking back to the condo after margaritas at the tiki bar, the heart sees a small crowd of people with red flashlights around one of the stone circles that guard the nests. As the heart kneels in the sand, the nest swells and bursts like a giant abscess and baby turtles scramble every which way, confused by the lights from the condos. Though the signs say you're not supposed to touch them, people pick up the wrong-pointed babies and set them off in the right direction like little matchbox cars. After watching hundreds of babies make their way to sea, the heart feels jubilant and tired, as if from giving birth itself. The next day the heart is despondent. *Striving, striving, is that all there is?* The heart wants to know.

The heart's favorite book? Heart of Darkness. Favorite song? Heart of Glass. Favorite band? I'll give you one guess.

The heart, on vacation, walks into one of those shops that does waxing, mani-pedis, threading, silk wraps, paraffin dips, eyeliner tattoos. A pedicure please, says the Heart. But—no toes, the proprietress points out indelicately. Just do your best, the heart reassures her in a voice pitched to assert a kind superiority, which at the end of the day will not go unpunished. The shop smells of vanilla-scented poison and burning keratin. A display of fake nails partially covers one wall, along with a painting of rainbow-hued horses bursting out of a diamond. The other wall is filled with shelves of tiny bottles of polish, from which the heart selects shocking pink. The spa chair punches the heart in odd places while it leafs through a fashion magazine. Finally, the heart thinks, a place to hide out for a while. They have to let it stay at least until the polish is dry.

Sometimes an evening comes along that turns you inside out like a dirty sock. The heart blanches to remember. What were their names? What were those drinks that tasted like grape soda and Valv-o-line? How efficient of memory to act as a strobe light does, illuminating every second frame, smoothing the night's edges by chopping it into bits. The last thing the heart remembers is the waiter from the karaoke bar pointing at his crotch and saying *necesito, por favor*. Also a motorcycle ride. And dancing with a Mexican butch who, in the middle of the dance floor, took off her foam rubber flip flop and used it to spank the heart's backside to a salsa rhythm. To its knowledge these scenes happen chronologically. Each scene whisks away the other until the heart wakes in its rented bed, with dried come in one ear, and in its hair.

The heart always goes down with the ship. That's what they say. But one of the lifeboats remains unaccounted for.

The heart returns to the office, the very site of unvariegated loneliness, to find the worker kitchen has been "greened" by a young upstart in personnel. Now, instead of styrofoam cups and little orange plastic stirs, there are unbleached paper cups and spindly wooden stirs. The creamer is still powdered, though, caked in its plastic trough. Rome wasn't built in a day.

In religious paintings, the heart leaving the body is depicted as a bird flying toward the sun. The heart is afraid of flying, having read the myth of Icarus. It prefers to inch along the sidewalk, tracing the crystal gleams of slugtrails.

The heart, walking through an up-scale neighborhood in a Midwest suburb, tired, hungry, and in need of a bath, sees a house where it appears no one is home. Actually, it's the house the heart grew up in, a place it dreams about, though in the dreams the house is usually in flames, the camellia bushes around it in flames, the first-kiss-porch-swing in flames. In the dream the heart runs up and down the stairs saving precious objects. It's like shopping only less stressful because the choices are made in a part of the heart's brain that slices quickly and surely, like a mandoline. These objects, the heart realizes, are the only true objects, reliquaries of memory. But it is difficult to pick them up with such short stumpy arms. In real life, the house is not on fire, just a little shabby looking. The heart approaches, goes around to the back, susses out the doggie door, looks around, gets down on all fours and climbs halfway through before getting stuck. An enormous dog trots into the kitchen and starts licking the heart's face.

The heart lies on a beach, slathered in coconut oil, imitation vintage transistor radio and a pack of Delicados by its side. The sea is an opalescent sheetcake frosted with occasional lazily cresting waves. Organisms known as devil worms can survive as deep as 2.2 miles beneath the earth's crust, the heart reads in a magazine. This information is startling enough, but what most tugs at the heart is the use of the word crust, the implication that every single thing on the surface of the earth—civilizations, edifices, canyons, flying buttresses, convenience stores, rivers, whiskey bars, drive-thru restaurants, landfills, golf courses, gated communities, mudflats, salt flats, health clubs, outlet stores, cemeteries, theme parks, water parks, apple orchards, pumpkin patches, savannahs, pyramids, jungles, deserts, factories, nuclear power plants, wind-harvesting plants, fruit-packing plants, wastewater treatment plants, crematoria, oceans, labyrinths, English gardens, parking lots, railroad ties, potato sheds, trailer parks, runways, peep shows, game shows, boardwalks, fishing piers, fine dining establishments, dog tracks, horse tracks, circuses, train tracks, wild game preserves, animal sanctuaries, war memorials, shellmounds, dance halls, sidewalks, border patrols, drive-thru daiquiri stands, buffalo herds, cornfields, wheat fields, rice paddies, Japanese gardens, Mayan temples, archipelagoes, gulags, steppes, moors, multiplexes, condos, highrises, bungalows, homeless shelters, underpasses, overpasses, cellphone towers, universities, think tanks, dams, reservoirs, penitentiaries, hospices, dude ranches, massage parlors, drive-thru wedding chapels, waterfalls, ski chalets, karaoke bars, rainforests, grazing lands, steakhouses, cancer wards, storefront churches, tattoo parlors, container stores, cathedrals, frescoes, discos, canals, wine cellars, termite mounds, leather bars, archery ranges, pilates studios, dungeons, unemployment offices, battlefields, VA hospitals, movie sets, botox clinics, sushi bars, drive-thru java huts, souvenir huts, pizza huts, quonset huts, airplane hangars, distilleries, heart clinics, white sand beaches—everything is just a crusted edge of skin, a thin scab momentarily formed over an eternal ooze. What plan or purpose can possibly lie in the earth's heart, its molten roiling core? A planet's heart is unfathomable, muses the heart, as am I.

The heart dreams it is St. Sebastian, festooned with arrows. What luck to have not been raised in the Catholic Church, and yet have access to all its pornography! In the dream the heart has a hard-on the size of a fist.

The heart thinks of its left auricle as its ample bosom, and of its right ventricle as its ammo box. When the heart jerks off it doesn't think about flesh at all, but pictures the sped up films of science class—flowers going from seed to sunburst in about ten seconds.

Auricle Atrium Auricle Atrium when one speaks the other listens you can actually hear much better with ears full of blood.

After another suitor disappoints the heart (don't say broken, never say broken) the heart takes up archery again, and is shocked by the paper targets one can now buy with images of people on them. You can practice shooting any kind of weapon at an African-American burglar, a generic white thug, or Osama Bin Laden. You cannot, at this range anyway, practice shooting George Bush, Sarah Palin, or Barack Obama. Even more upsetting to the heart than the human targets are the silhouettes of wolves, rabbits, and crows with crosshairs placed over their vulnerable areas. The heart is interested in the symbolism of archery, in the physics of flight, in precision and mastery for its own sake, and would like to forget certain practical applications.

The heart howls in the street like an ambulance caught in a traffic jam, or like a tender animal caught in the maw of a larger, fiercer animal. The heart howls so loudly and for so long that it is amazing that no one has ears sensitive enough to hear it. Just like we wait for evolution to invent an organism that can digest plastic,* the heart awaits an instrument sophisticated enough to measure its screams. Like a child "allowed" to cry itself out in its bedroom, the heart eventually exhausts all sadness, all grief, all operatic terror, and sinks from its spasms to a place of low comfort.

*Actually, this organism has been discovered, a fungus in the Amazon, is being studied as we speak. It remains to be seen what this discovery will mean for humanity's penchant for trashing the world.

The heart lies buried in silt at the bottom of the sea. What was once a dumb valve for pumping juice turns out to be a black box bearing evidence into a future one hopes will understand it. We who care about the heart memorize its coordinates and pass them down. One day hearts will form an underwater ring, rise from ancient sea beds draped in the songs of a thousand Atlantises. Hearts wait for technology to catch up to them, decode their lapses. But hearts can't wait forever. They float to the surface and bob to the nearest atoll. They write tell-all memoirs in their heads, and practice signing autographs in the sand.

The heart inserts the metal fitting into the buckle, then pulls the strap away from the buckle to adjust the belt low and tight across its waist. The heart orders a snack box for ten dollars, containing some pita chips and a triangular pillow of grainy hummus. The heart picks items out of the catalog that never changes—what the heart wants from this catalog never changes either: the curved body pillow, the silk sleep sack, and the fake rocks for hiding eyesores in the yard, though the heart has no yard. The heart would put the rocks in other people's yards as a joke, hiding very small things under them, like origami animals, plastic fruit, and Barbie telephones. Or even a real telephone, which would ring while a person was doing yard work and they would look around the yard and think, Is that rock ringing? And sure enough, they would walk over to the rock and touch its thin fiberglass cone-like head, lift its shell to see the phone lying there in the dirt, lit up with ringtone, something jazzy and insistent. Hello, the person would say. Hello, the heart would say from its hiding place across the street and behind a bush. This is the heart calling. And everything would go from there.

Acknowledgements

This book was written at the RADAR Lab in Akumal, Mexico, thanks to Michelle Tea, Ali Liebegott, Beth Pickens, and my fellow lab rats. Thanks are also very much due to the San Francisco Arts Commission, Lucy Corin, Rainbow Grocery, and my family.